THE NEW NINJA

By Meredith Rusu

M SCHOLASTIC

Scholastic Children's Books
Euston House,
24 Eversholt Street,
London NW1 1DB, UK

A division of Scholastic Ltd
London ~ New York ~ Toronto ~ Sydney ~ Auckland
Mexico City ~ New Delhi ~ Hong Kong

This book was first published in the US in 2016 by Scholastic Inc.
Published in the UK by Scholastic Ltd, 2016

ISBN 978 1407 16224 9

Printed and bound by CPI Group (UK) Ltd, Croydon, CR0 4YY

2 4 6 8 10 9 7 5 3 1

www.scholastic.co.uk

MIX
Paper from
responsible sources
FSC® C020471

FROM THE JOURNAL OF

Sensei Wu

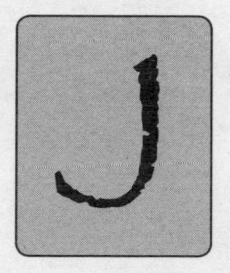ust as the water ebbs and flows with the ocean's tide, so, too, has Ninjago™ seen evil ebb and flow from its shores. All seemed lost when Morro – a vengeful ghost and my former pupil – escaped from the Cursed Realm. He gained control of the Realm Crystal and unleashed a powerful monster unlike any Ninjago had ever seen: the Preeminent. This terrible beast contained the Cursed Realm inside it. Once unleashed, it threatened to consume Ninjago and all the sixteen realms forever.

Yet when the tide of evil seemed too much for even the ninja to overcome, a new hero arose: Nya. As the Master of Water, she had the ability to destroy the Preeminent, as water is the only weapon against which ghosts are powerless.

But the Preeminent was strong. Even the ocean was not deep enough to stop it. Nya needed to unlock her true potential to create a wall of water powerful enough to defeat the beast. And in the final battle, she did just that. Ninjago was safe once more.

Now Cole, Jay, Kai, Lloyd and Zane have a new ninja by their side. And yet, I wonder. Is Nya prepared for the challenges that she will face as a ninja?

I do not worry about her strength, but rather her independence. Nya has always been an important part of the team, and yet in many ways she has always been

separate from the others. She has come to the team's aid many times as Samurai X, but always on her own terms. Being a true team member requires not just individual strength, but the confidence to know when group strength is required.

By unlocking her true potential, Nya proved herself worthy as a ninja. Will she succeed now as she steps forward to join the others? I believe that she will. But time is the only master that can answer this question . . .

Chapter 1

ya, I need your help!"

It was Cole. He was in trouble!

"Just a second!" Nya raced ahead as fast as she could.

"Nya – a little help please?" This time, it was Kai.

"Stand by!" Nya shouted. She was almost there!

"Nya, we're in the *other* direction," Kai exclaimed. "Where are you going?"

"Just one ... more ... second ..."

DUN DA DUN! The video game in front of them played a victory melody. "Record delivery score ACHIEVED!"

"Yes!" Nya pumped her fist. She had delivered her final video game pizza in the nick of time. She'd beaten her own personal record – thirty-two pizzas in under three minutes! Now she could go and help Kai and Cole.

But as she turned around . . .

KA-BOOM!

"Ha! **Gotcha!** " Jay exclaimed.

The screen displayed a bright explosion of colours as Kai's and Cole's delivery trucks were destroyed. Their avatars spun upside down, and their eyes turned into little Xs.

GAME OVER, the television screen announced.

"Zane and I win!" Jay cheered, doing a silly dance. "Score another round for team Pizza-Go!"

8

Cole, Jay, Kai, Nya and Zane were seated around an oversized television screen onboard the *Destiny's Bounty*. They were playing Ninjago's most popular new video game: *Delivery Trucks vs. Zombies: Pizza Party of Doom.*

Cole, Kai and Nya were on one team, while Jay and Zane were on the other. Each team was supposed to deliver as many pizzas as they could before the zombies caught up with them. But every time they played, Jay used his pepperoni cannon to stop Kai's and Cole's delivery trucks. For seventeen games in a row.

Kai grumbled as digitized zombies carried his and Cole's avatars offscreen. "Look, sis." He turned to Nya. "We can only win if we work together."

"But I delivered all my pizzas," Nya insisted. "In record time!"

"Yeah, but Jay keeps stopping *us* from delivering any of *our* pizzas," Kai said.

Nya shrugged. "I can't help it that Jay has become so good at this game. Ever since we defeated the Preeminent, he's spent twelve hours a day playing *Delivery Trucks vs. Zombies.*"

"Thirteen hours, twenty-seven minutes and thirty-two seconds a day, to be precise," Zane noted.

Jay beamed. "What can I say? **Ninja never quit!** And that includes video games."

Kai shook his head. "Nya, the point of the game is that we have to deliver the most pizzas *as a team*. That's the only way to win. You're a ninja now. We work together in everything. Even in video games."

"All right, all right," Nya said. "Let's play another round. This time, I'll make sure I've got you guys' backs." She winked. "*And* I'll beat my personal record again."

Cole nudged Kai. "It would help if Jay stopped targeting *our* delivery trucks and

went after Nya once in a while."

Jay gulped.

Nya's cheeks turned bright red. "What's *that* supposed to mean?"

Not long ago, Nya and Jay had kind of, sort of been a couple. But now that she was the Master of Water, Nya wasn't sure how she felt. Between training with Sensei Wu and unlocking her true potential *and* saving all of Ninjago from destruction (again), she had a lot on her mind. For now, she just wanted to focus on being a ninja.

"I already told you guys," Nya said. "Jay and I are just friends. It's *never* going to happen."

She didn't mean for her words to come out so harshly. A hurt look crossed Jay's face. But none of the other ninja noticed.

"Anyway . . ." Jay said, quickly changing the subject. "Do you think the kids at the hospital will like *Delivery Trucks vs. Zombies* as the finale to our 'Ninja for a

Day' video game tournament?"

"They're gonna love it!" Cole exclaimed. He grabbed a gooey slice of pizza from a box on the floor. "It's gaming. It's pizza. It's zombies. What's not to love?"

Cole was right. The kids at the hospital were sure to be very excited about the event, and not just because of the video game fun. Ever since the ninja had defeated the Preeminent, they had become celebrities around New Ninjago. Their friend Dareth had even offered to be their agent. As Dareth had said, "You need someone to navigate you through the sticky waters of celebrity. And I, Dareth, award-winning karate master, owner of Dareth's Mojo Dojo, and the legendary **Brown Ninja**, will be your guide."

For the most part, the ninja didn't really want to be in the limelight. But when Dareth suggested they host a "Ninja for a Day"

programme to cheer up the kids in the hospital, everyone agreed it sounded like a great idea. This weekend was the kickoff event, ending with a video game tournament to determine the ultimate Ninja for a Day.

"It was pretty cool of Dareth to set it up," said Nya. "Even if it's only because he wants to make us more famous."

"I wonder how Lloyd is doing with the set-up down at the hospital," Jay said, grabbing a slice of pizza for himself.

Suddenly, lights began flashing on the bridge. An **urgent message** was coming in for the ninja!

"Hold that thought," Kai exclaimed. "Looks like it's go time!"

Chapter 2

"**G**uys, come in. Can you hear me?"

Lloyd's voice came through the intercom as the ninja raced onto the bridge.

"Lloyd, is that you?" Kai asked, switching on the monitor.

"What is it?" Jay asked eagerly. "Is there danger? Action? Trouble? An army of bad guys for us to take down?"

Lloyd shook his head. "Not exactly. But I do need your help." He shifted the camera to show a group of hospital children behind

him. They were going **bananas**. Despite their casts and bandages, the kids were gathering around an enormous stack of crates.

"Dareth went overboard with the 'Ninja for a Day' giveaways," Lloyd explained. "There are fifty crates of ninja action figures here. And the kids found them . . ."

Lloyd ducked as something flew over his head.

"*Oooh*, was that a Kai action figure I just saw go by?" Kai asked, trying to keep the excitement out of his voice.

"Not another box of red ones!" A kid's disappointed voice wailed over the intercom. "Where are all the Green Ninja? **WHERE?**"

"Aw." Kai sighed.

Lloyd turned the camera back on himself. "Can you guys come down here to help me get these crates away and finish setting up?"

"Of course," said Zane. "We will even bring the video game system for installation. See you soon."

As Lloyd disconnected the call, the game console behind Cole, Jay, Kai, Nya and Zane sparked. **PFFFZZZZZZt!**

"That didn't sound good," said Jay.

"It's okay." Nya grabbed her box of computer tools. "I had to tinker with the operating board when I interconnected all the video games for the tournament. There's probably just a quick bug to fix. You guys go help Lloyd. I'll work on the console and bring it over in a flash."

"Oh, okay." Jay watched as Nya got to work. "You sure you don't need any help? I'm pretty handy when it comes to fixing things. I grew up in a junkyard, after all."

Nya shook her head. "I'm fine. I got this."

Half an hour later, Nya was humming as she finished rewiring the video game console.

"Hello? Can anyone hear us?"

Nya wheeled out from beneath the console and lifted her goggles. "Hello?" she called. "Who's there?"

"Oh, they can hear us, Edna!"

"Very good, dear. Tell them we need help!"

It was Jay's parents, Ed and Edna, calling the *Destiny's Bounty*. Nya hurried to the bridge.

"Is everything okay?" she asked.

"Oh, hello, Nya!" Edna brightened when she saw her. "How are you doing, dear? Is Jay there?"

Nya shook her head. "It's just me. The others are down at the children's hospital helping set up for 'Ninja for a Day'."

"Oh, dear," said Edna. "We were hoping you all might be able to come."

"You see, we're in a **bit of a pickle**," Ed added.

The screen suddenly went fuzzy. When it came back on, Jay's parents were gone. Instead, a Nindroid was walking straight towards the camera!

"Terminate . . . terminate!" it repeated.

"Ed! Edna!" Nya called.

There was no answer. A moment later, the screen went black.

Nya gasped. Jay's parents were in trouble! She had to get to the junkyard.

"No time to call the others," Nya declared, lowering the hood of her gi. "I'm a ninja now, and ninja take care of business. Like Kai said . . . **It's go time!**"

Chapter 3

Nya skidded up to the entrance of Ed and Edna's Scrap n Junk, kicking up a cloud of dust as her DBX flyer screeched to a halt. She leaped out of the driver's seat.

"Ed! Edna!" she called. "Where are you?"

"Terminate! Terminate!"

Nindroid voices echoed from every corner. Nya ran through the gates and gasped. A large conveyor belt in the centre of the junkyard was running all the way up a tower of rubble. At least a dozen Nindroids

were swarming around the bottom of the belt. And Ed and Edna were trapped at the top!

"Oh, look, Ed!" Edna pointed at the ground. "It's Nya!"

"Hiya, Nya!" Ed called down. "Are the boys with you?"

"No – it's just me," Nya said. She narrowed her eyes at the Nindroids. "But don't worry. I'm a fully-fledged ninja now. I'll take care of these Nindroids, no sweat."

"Oh, well, you see . . ." Edna started.

But Nya didn't hear her. "*Ninja-GO!*" she cried.

With a running leap, Nya bounded right on top of the first Nindroid's head! "Mind if I step in?" she quipped. Using the first Nindroid to propel her, she bounced from one to the next. One . . . two . . . three . . . she knocked them down like a row of dominoes. **"Hi-ya!"** Nya flipped into an awesome kick, taking

down another two Nindroids. "I can see why the guys are always eager for action," she said with a confident smile. "This is fun!"

Suddenly, seven more Nindroids swarmed out of the junkyard workshop. "Terminate! Terminate!"

"Looks like you guys need to cool off," Nya said. Taking a deep breath, she closed her eyes.

"Nya, dear!" Edna called down. "I don't think you understand . . ."

But Nya was too focused on summoning her elemental powers to hear. Dark clouds appeared overhead. There was a big **whoosh**, and a wall of rainwater poured down.

The Nindroids sizzled and sparked. "Terminate . . . *terrrrrrrmmmmmiinnnnnnn . . .*"

The Nindroids shut down.

"Well, that takes care of that," Nya said, pleased with herself.

Suddenly, she heard a rumbling behind her.

The force of the storm was too strong for the mountain of rubble. It was starting to collapse!

"Oh, no," Nya exclaimed. "Hang on, guys!"

Nya took a deep breath, and then concentrated on forming a big pool of rainwater. As the pile of debris collapsed, Ed and Edna splashed safely into the water. A moment later, they popped up, soaked through.

"Sorry about that," Nya apologized. "But hey, I took care of those Nindroids pretty well, right? Are you guys okay?"

Ed wiped off his glasses. "You sure did, **you betcha**! You're one strong ninja. Too bad I'll have to repair them, though . . ."

Ed looked at the bent and twisted conveyor belt that had collapsed along with the pile of junk. "And my new conveyor belt."

"Huh?" Nya asked, confused.

"You see, dear, those Nindroids were helping us," Edna explained. "Ed here managed to rewire them after the Digital Overlord days—"

"Whew, those were a doozy!" Ed said.

"And they were doing chores around the junkyard," Edna continued. "We built this new conveyor belt to stack spare parts, but we got stuck at the top."

"Those Nindroids were helpful, but they weren't the brightest," Ed said. "They knew they needed to 'terminate' the conveyor belt from going up so we could climb down. But they didn't know how to turn it off."

"We were hoping the boys could use their **Air-u-jitzu-witzu** to get us down," Edna said. "And that Zane could reprogramme the Nindroids to be a bit, well, smarter."

"*Ohhhhhhhh . . .*" Nya looked around at

the mess she'd made in the junkyard. Her face fell.

"It's okay." Ed patted her shoulder. "Nothing we can't fix. And hey, those were some **pretty** nifty **ninja moves** you showed off there!"

"Thanks." Nya rubbed the back of her neck, embarrassed. "Do you mind doing me a favour, though? Don't tell the boys. They'll never let me hear the end of this."

Chapter 4

The next day, Lloyd sat cross-legged in the middle of the *Destiny's Bounty*. The other ninja had prepared an obstacle course filled with training dummies to help with his sensei training.

"We're on top of a mountain," Kai told Lloyd. "And we're faced with an army of skeleton warriors."

"We're surrounded," said Zane. "What would a sensei tell us to do?"

"Um . . ." Lloyd thought. "He'd probably tell you to **make some tea** ."

Kai grinned. "Ready, sis?"

Nya nodded. "You know it!"

Nya sent a blast of water straight at Kai, who used his fire power to heat the water into steam. Instantly, the training course was shrouded in a **thick, white cloud** . The sound of dummies being pummelled echoed through the ship. When the steam cleared, the ninja had taken out all the dummies in one shot!

"Nice job, Sensei," Jay said to Lloyd.

"Yes, that was indeed sound advice," Zane said. "Worthy of Sensei Garmadon himself."

"Thanks, guys." Lloyd smiled a bit sadly and looked down at his gi. It was his father's. In order to save Ninjago, Sensei Garmadon had stayed trapped inside the Cursed Realm. When the ninja destroyed the Preeminent, the Cursed Realm had been lost along with the beast.

Lloyd didn't know where his father was

now. But he liked to think that one day they'd be together again.

"I miss my dad," Lloyd admitted. "But I think he'd be proud."

Suddenly, the lights on the bridge lit up. Another message was coming in for the ninja.

Cole sighed. "I guess we'll have to put Lloyd's training on hold. Again."

Nya jumped up. "You guys keep practising. I'll go see who it is. It's probably just Dareth letting us know about another publicity stunt or something."

Nya hurried to the bridge. She was right — it was Dareth calling. But he wasn't calling about publicity.

"It's out of control down here!" he cried through the intercom. "I'm at Ninjago Film Industries. **Big trouble! Massive trouble!** We need the ninja!"

"Are you sure?" Nya asked doubtfully.

This wouldn't be the first time Dareth had called the ninja insisting there was trouble, only for them to show up and find a camera crew waiting for an interview. "Is this another publicity stunt?"

Dareth shook his head. "I swear, this time it's real. We're on the set filming an unauthorized documentary, *Way of the Ninja: The Rise of Ninjago's Greatest Heroes*. But things have gone *bad*. See for yourself!"

Dareth turned his phone's screen to show the scene behind him. Kruncha and Nuckal, two skeleton warriors, were there, arguing loudly with the crew.

"I told you, *intern*." Kruncha knocked a tray of drinks out of a young studio aide's hands. "No pulp in my orange juice! And you!" Kruncha whirled on the movie's director. "How dare you cast us as extras?! Don't you know who we are?"

"Yeah!" Nuckal said. "Don't you know

who we are?" A blank look suddenly crossed his face. "Uh, who are we again?"

Kruncha bopped Nuckal on the head. "We're two of the most feared skeleton warriors in Ninjago. We deserve to be cast as leads in this movie!"

The skeletons clomped around, knocking over props and yelling at everyone in their path.

Dareth came back onscreen. "Nya, we really need you and the boys down here!"

"Okay, Dareth," Nya said. "We'll be right there."

Nya hurried back out to the training course to get the others. But when she got there, she paused.

The other ninja were really focused on training Lloyd. She hated to interrupt them. It was important for Lloyd to master his sensei training. More important than stopping two **unruly** skeletons on the set of Dareth's silly movie.

And besides . . . a little part of Nya wanted to handle this problem herself. Even though she'd made a bit of a mess at the junkyard, using her new ninja abilities had been pretty awesome. Two skeletons were no big deal. She could easily stop them from making trouble and let the others continue training Lloyd.

I'll be there and back before they even notice I'm gone, Nya said to herself with a smile.

But when Nya reached Ninjago Film Industries, she couldn't believe her eyes. The set was in chaos!

Extras in skeleton costumes were running back and forth wildly, while a group of actors in stone warrior outfits were having a food fight at one of the lunch buffet tables. Props were knocked over. Film reels were

scattered everywhere. And all the while, the director was frantically calling, "**Cut! Cut!**"

"What happened?" Nya asked Dareth as she hopped out of the DBX flyer.

"It was awful," Dareth wailed. "Nuckal and Kruncha ... They started a riot! The cast all demanded higher pay. Better food. And then, they did the *unthinkable*."

"What?" Nya asked, worried. Maybe she should have asked the other ninja to come along after all. "What did they do? Was anyone hurt?"

"**Worse,**" moaned Dareth dramatically. "They ... they ..."

"What?!" Nya demanded.

"They took the film reel! All that work ... gone!"

Nya rolled her eyes. "Ugh. Okay, I'll handle them. Where are they now?"

Dareth sobbed. "Who can say? The costume department? The parking lot?

They could be right behind us for all we know!"

"Right behind us ..." Nya repeated slowly.

From behind her, the DBX flyer's engine revved loudly.

"Heh, heh, heh."

"Oh, no." Nya groaned.

Kruncha and Nuckal were behind the wheel, dressed up in ninja costumes from the movie set.

"We'll show them who the *real* stars of this film are!" Kruncha exclaimed. **"It's joyride time!"**

Chapter 5

This was an epic disaster. Nuckal and Kruncha were disguised as ninja, and they were stealing the DBX flyer!

"Stop!" Nya cried.

"Oh, look." Nuckal snickered. "It's the *girl* ninja."

"What's the matter?" Kruncha asked. "Are two skeletons too much for the *girl* ninja to handle?"

Now Nya was really angry. "I'll show you who's too much to handle!" she shouted.

That only made the skeletons laugh

harder. With another rev of the engine, they sped away.

"Quick, Dareth, I need a vehicle," Nya exclaimed.

Dareth shook his head. "All we have are movie props! The film version of the DBX flyer doesn't even have a real engine."

He pointed to a clunky replica of the DBX flyer across the set. It was built out of cheap metal and had a bad paint job. But it did have wheels and an exhaust pipe.

Nya grinned. "That'll work!"

In a flash, she hopped in. Using her elemental power, she shot a stream of water out through the fake DBX flyer's exhaust pipe, propelling it forward.

"Hold on to your costumes, skeletons!" Nya said. "You're about to face **a real ninja** with water power."

Nya shot after Nuckal and Kruncha, chasing them through downtown. The skeletons zipped around corners and

through crowded intersections. But that wasn't going to stop Nya! She matched them turn for turn, careening over bumps and weaving in and out of traffic.

"Give it up, you two!" she shouted.

The skeletons laughed. "Ninja skeletons never quit!"

Stepping on the gas, they zoomed down the street. They were heading straight for New Ninjago Bay.

Perfect! thought Nya. That gave her an idea . . .

Nya veered to the left and over a small bridge across an inlet of water. In a moment, she was out of sight.

The two skeletons looked behind them.

"Ha." Kruncha laughed. "Looks like the girl ninja isn't as tough as she thought. She couldn't even catch her own vehicle."

"Yeah." Nuckal laughed. "Not so tough!"

"Time to see what this bad boy can really

do!" Kruncha put his bony foot on the gas. Pedestrians scurried left and right out of the vehicle's path. The DBX flyer zipped forward. Trees and buildings whizzed by. They were going at top speed, sailing past New Ninjago Bay, when suddenly . . .

WHOOSH!

A giant wave of water rose up from the bay and scooped up the renegade DBX flyer! With an enormous *splash*, the vehicle toppled upside down, screeching to a halt at the centre of the plaza next to the bay. Nuckal and Kruncha spilled out, somersaulting to a stop at Nya's feet.

Nya smiled victoriously. "Didn't anyone ever warn you not to mess with me in *my* element?"

The two waterlogged skeletons groaned.

"We just wanted to be in the movie," Nuckal whined.

Suddenly, the sound of a helicopter thundered overhead. It was Dareth!

"Cut!" he called through a megaphone. He dropped a ladder down from the helicopter and climbed to the ground. "That. Was. Incredible! We caught it all on film! It's going to be perfect in the unauthorized documentary!"

The skeletons gasped. "You mean... we're stars?!"

Dareth adjusted his sunglasses. "That was great, Nya baby. So much chaos. So much destruction. The fans will eat it up!"

"Chaos? Destruction?" Nya asked.

She looked back over the path she'd taken in pursuit of Nuckal and Kruncha. The streets downtown were a mess. Food stalls were toppled over. Lamp posts were knocked askew. Some citizens stared with mouths gaping, while others looked... well... pretty annoyed.

A little girl came up to Nya and tugged on her gi.

"That was crazy!" She gave Nya a

gap-toothed grin. "Where are the other ninja?"

"Yeah," a small boy chimed in. "You stopped the skeletons with water! Do you think Zane could have frozen the DBX flyer's wheels?"

"Uh . . ." said Nya.

"Or that Lloyd could have used his Green Ninja power to keep the truck from hitting all those food stalls?" the little girl asked.

"Well . . ." Nya said.

"Or that Jay could have used his lightning to overload the engine's circuits?"

Nya sighed. The kids were right. The other ninja could have done all those things. And probably could have made a lot less mess while they were doing them, too.

But hey, she *had* stopped the skeletons, right? After all, she was the Ninja of Water. It was her job to solve problems her way, using her element.

Wasn't it?

Chapter 6

Exhausted, Nya made her way back to the *Destiny's Bounty*. When she arrived, she found a note from the ninja.

Nya – we're heading downtown for noodles. Team dinner! Come and join us when you get back.

Nya smiled. The guys had always treated her like one of the gang. And now that she was the Master of Water, being on the team felt even more special.

And different. If she was being completely honest, Nya sometimes missed the solo

excitement of being Samurai X. Doing things her own way, saving the day in secret — that was familiar. As cool as it was to be the Master of Water, it was a big change.

Nya sighed as she reached the bridge. Misako was there, working on a computer.

"Hi, Misako," Nya said. "Did the guys leave a long time ago?"

Misako shook her head. "Just twenty minutes ago."

"Thanks." Nya plopped into a chair. "*Whew*, I guess all that excitement downtown tired me out."

"**Excitement downtown?**" Misako asked. "The boys didn't mention anything."

Nya waved her hand. "Oh, it was just Nuckal and Kruncha. Those two boneheads were causing trouble at Ninjago Film Industries. I went to stop them, and then they stole the DBX flyer and . . . well, it caused a bit of a mess. But I took care of

them." Nya smiled proudly. "Next time they'll think twice before messing with water."

To Nya's surprise, Misako seemed worried. "Was anyone hurt?"

Nya shook her head. "Oh, no, no. Well, a few food stalls were knocked over. It was nothing like the mess at Jay's parents' junkyard yesterday."

"Something happened at the junkyard?" asked Misako, raising an eyebrow.

Oops. Nya hadn't been planning to tell anyone about that.

"Oh . . . uh, nothing bad. Ed and Edna are fine," Nya assured her. "It was just a couple of Nindroids that Jay's dad had rewired. I thought they were attacking, so I used my water power to stop them. But it turns out they were just helping Ed and Edna. I made a bit of a mess at the junkyard. And I broke Ed's conveyor belt. But hey, Ed said my ninja skills were pretty impressive."

"I don't understand. Where were the

other ninja?" Misako asked, confused. "Why didn't they help you?"

"Well . . . I didn't exactly tell them," Nya admitted. "They were busy setting up at the hospital and then training Lloyd – I didn't want to bother them. Besides, the problems weren't anything I couldn't handle. At least, they seemed like they weren't at the time . . ."

A knowing look crossed Misako's face. "I'm sure you handled them just fine. But, Nya, sometimes our **greatest strength** comes when we accept the strength of others. You and the ninja are a team now, even more so than before. You are at your best when you **work together**."

Nya looked down. "I know. I wasn't trying to show off or anything. I just thought that was what I was supposed to do. I mean, that's my job now, right? This being a ninja thing doesn't come with a job description! But I'm the Master of Water. I'm a ninja."

"And you are also a member of the team," said Misako. "That may be your greatest power of all."

A few minutes later, Nya headed downtown to meet the guys. She was thinking about what Misako had said. Nya felt a little bad for not telling the rest of the team about the two calls for help when they came in. She would tell them about her misadventures when she saw them. She didn't want to keep secrets from them. From now on, she would try harder to work together with the others.

Suddenly, something caught her eye. An oversized television screen displayed the news on the side of a building. Helicopter crews were filming in real time, hovering over the village of Stiix (or what was left of it, after all the destruction the Preeminent had caused).

"This is Fred Finely, coming to you live from Stiix," the news reporter announced. "It seems trouble has returned to Ninjago! As you're seeing here first, on Ninjago Channel 8 – the Nocho – ghosts once again walk among us! Two sightings have been reported in Stiix over the past few hours. What does this mean for Ninjago? Is the Preeminent truly gone? Most importantly, **where are the ninja?"**

The screen changed to footage of two ghosts making mischief on the streets of Stiix. Residents who had just started to rebuild their city ran terrified from the creatures.

Nya gasped. "I can't believe it. Ghosts? But how?" She thought fast. "If I go right now, I can stop them. I have water power – that's the only thing that ghosts are powerless against!" Nya paused. "But I should get the others. Like Misako said, we're strongest together."

Quickly, Nya pressed the communicator button on the DBX flyer. "Guys, come in. There's trouble!"

Bzzzzzzt! Nothing but static.

Nya looked in dismay at the hanging wires from the communicator panel. "What did Nuckal and Kruncha *do* to this thing?"

She reached into her pocket for her mobile phone.

But it was empty.

"*And* I left my phone back at the *Destiny's Bounty*? Perfect."

Nya watched in alarm as the ghosts on the television screen chased the people of Stiix.

"Those people need help now," she said. "If I go to get the guys, it could be too late. Or . . ."

Suddenly, she had an **idea**.

Nya lowered the driver's side window and called out to an elderly couple on the street.

"Quick, I need your help!" she said. "Please, go to the noodle shop downtown. The ninja are there. Tell them to hurry to Stiix. Ghosts are on the loose! Tell them Nya will already be there."

The old couple nodded. "Of course, dear!"

"Thank you. Thank you so much!" In a cloud of dust, Nya made a **giant U-turn** and headed towards Stiix.

The old man turned to his wife. "Where are we supposed to go now, Mildred?"

"Didn't you hear, Ernest? To the poodle shop downtown. The ninja are there!"

"*Oooh*, the ninja." Ernest pulled a Kai action figure out from his pocket. "I've always wanted to meet them. Maybe they'll autograph my action figure!"

Chapter 7

ya screeched across the bridge to Stiix. Terrified citizens scurried past her on their way out of town.

"Where are the ghosts?" she asked a fleeing woman.

"At the Food Market," the woman shouted. "They're eating everything in sight!"

Nya remembered how the ghosts had been super-hungry when they'd first attacked Stiix. "Don't worry. I'll give them something to chew on!"

Nya sped down the block. When she reached the Food Market, she could hear the sounds of shattering glass and breaking wood. Ghostly green light shone through the store's windows.

Stealthily, Nya made her way inside. She crept up behind a large pile of crates. Two ghosts were floating just a few feet away, chowing down.

"Om nom nom," one ghost said.

"They just don't make burgers like this in the Cursed Realm," the other replied.

Nya smiled. "How about a little something to wash those burgers down?" In a flash, she shot a blast of water out at one of the ghosts. Direct hit! The ghost vanished in a puff of green vapour.

Its partner looked up and hissed. "It's the Ninja of Water!"

Suddenly, something smacked Nya from behind – hard. "Ow!"

She fell to the floor, dazed. As she rolled away, she spotted a third ghost hovering overhead. It was coming down to attack! **"Oh, no, you don't!"** Nya said. She sent an entire stack of water jugs flying at the ghost. It dodged, and the jugs splattered across the wall behind it.

"We must go!" the ghost shouted to its friend. Together, they *zoomed* out of the store.

"You can't get away that easily," Nya exclaimed. She sprinted after them through the deserted streets of Stiix. Helicopter lights shone down from the news reporters above, creating eerie shadows all around her.

Nya whipped around a corner – now there were three ghosts! She shot another blast of water.

FWOOSH!

One ghost vanished. But there were still two left.

"This way!" the ghost hissed to its partner.

Nya chased after them, weaving in and out of rubble-filled city streets. She panted as she ran. The other ninja would be there soon. Like Misako said, she would have her team to back her up.

Unless I'm able to take these ghouls down all on my own, Nya thought.

At the city centre, the ghosts suddenly flew straight up, heading to the top of the tallest tower in Stiix.

Nya caught her breath and frowned. She didn't know Airjitzu yet. "Looks like I'm climbing," she huffed.

With a **fresh burst of speed**, Nya took the stairs two at a time. She climbed up, up, up. At the top of the tower, she found herself atop a large roof surrounded by an ornate railing. From here, she could see the entire village.

The two ghosts hovered directly overhead.

"Ready to surrender?" Nya said, powering up a spinning ball of water. "Your time is up."

To her surprise, the ghosts just laughed. "It is you whose time is up," the first ghost said, leering at her.

Suddenly, an **eerie green glow** appeared from behind the tower. Nya gasped as an entire army of ghosts rose up into the sky. There had to be thirty of them – maybe more. And they were all ready to attack.

Nya slowly backed away, water ball still spinning.

"I don't understand," she said. "How did you escape from the Cursed Realm? There isn't even a Cursed Realm any more – I destroyed it!"

"Escape – no escape," the lead ghost hissed. "We did not get trapped when the Cursed Realm fell."

"We hid, waiting for our time," another

ghost cackled. "Now there is no Cursed Realm for us. Only this realm."

"And this village," the first ghost rasped. "It is under our control now."

Nya narrowed her eyes. "Not if I have anything to say about it."

The ghosts howled. "Yes – only one stands in our way. The Ninja of Water. The one who defeated the Preeminent. If we defeat her, then we are invincible!"

Nya made her ball of water even larger. "Too bad, because you're about to go down."

An evil smile crossed the lead ghost's face. "Down," it jeered. "Not for us, but for the Ninja of Water. She is strong, but can she fly?"

The ghost shrieked as it swooped towards her. Nya dodged to the left, shooting her water ball full blast at the ghosts. She vapourized one ghost, but three more were right behind it.

With a sinking feeling, Nya realized there were too many of them. The ghosts had led her to the tower on purpose! She could hold them off for a while, but without Airjitzu, she was trapped. And in **big trouble**.

She needed help to win this battle. She needed the other ninja!

Where *were* they? Why hadn't they come yet?

Chapter 8

Man, these noodles are sooooooo good!" Cole said with a loud *slurp*. "Guys, I think becoming a ghost has made me even hungrier."

"I'm not sure that's possible," Kai joked. "But it may have given you a bottomless stomach."

The ninja laughed while Cole shook his head. "Very funny. But seriously, Jay, are you going to finish your noodles? Or can I have them?"

Jay didn't answer. He tapped his

chopsticks on the table, looking out the door.

"Uh, Earth to Jay," said Kai. **"Are you okay?"**

"Yes," said Zane. "Your appetite seems significantly decreased."

"Something on your mind?" asked Lloyd.

Jay shook his head. "It's just . . . Shouldn't Nya have been here by now? Maybe we should have waited for her."

Kai frowned. "Now that you mention it, it is weird she hasn't joined us. Do any of you know where she went while we were training Lloyd?"

The others shook their heads.

"Maybe we should check to make sure she's okay," Kai said.

The guys buzzed Nya's phone. But Misako answered it.

"Hello, boys," she said. "Are you and Nya enjoying your noodles?"

"Actually, Nya isn't here," said Kai. "We

were calling to see where she was."

"She accidentally left her phone on the *Destiny's Bounty*," Misako said. "She isn't there yet? That's . . . odd. She left nearly an hour ago."

Suddenly, a customer rushed into the noodle shop. "Turn on the television!" he exclaimed. "You've *got* to see what's happening in Stiix!"

A waiter flicked on the television at the front of the restaurant. Everyone watched wide-eyed as the news came on.

"This just in," announced Fred Finely. "Reporting to you live from Stiix, Nya the Water Ninja is taking on twenty – no, thirty! – ghosts single-handedly. You're seeing it here first, folks. Nya is cornered on the tallest tower in Stiix, and she's fighting off an army of ghosts! Can she hold them off?"

Jay's chopsticks fell to the floor with a clatter. Before anyone had time to cry *Ninja-GO!*, Cole, Jay, Kai, Lloyd and Zane

had dashed out of the noodle shop and summoned their elemental dragons.

A moment later, the restaurant's door bells jingled. It was the elderly couple Nya had spoken to earlier.

"Can anyone tell us where the poodle shop is?" they asked. "We have an **urgent message** for the ninja."

Chapter 9

"**U***hggh!*" Nya grunted as she shot out three consecutive water blasts. They were powerful, but all way off target. Every time she tried to aim, ghosts would dive-bomb her. There wasn't even enough time to focus and start a rainstorm. She had to keep dodging and rolling just to avoid being knocked off the tower.

Suddenly, one of the ghosts lashed a possessed chain at her. Nya leaped away just in the nick of time.

Clang! The chain hit a pipe on the roof,

possessing it, too!

Breathing hard, Nya ducked behind a utility wall. "I really wish the guys would get here," she said. "They sure are taking their sweet time."

But deep down, Nya realized she was in big trouble. She'd jumped the gun again, running off without the other ninja. There was no way of knowing if that elderly couple had given her message to Cole, Jay, Kai, Lloyd and Zane. They might not be on their way at all.

Nya should have gone herself to get the guys. Then they could have arrived as a team. **At their strongest.**

But she couldn't worry about that now. The ghosts were getting closer, gearing up for another attack. She had to keep fighting them off until she figured out a plan.

"Hi-ya!" Nya leaped from behind the wall and unleashed her fastest water barrage yet. One, two, three, four! Water flew in every

direction. She clipped a lot of ghosts. But somehow, more just kept coming.

Nya backed against the rail of the tower. The wind whipped past her as news helicopters filmed the action from a distance.

Nya looked out to the news choppers. "Kai, Cole, Lloyd, Jay, Zane," she shouted as loudly as she could to the cameras. "If you're seeing this, I could really use back-up right about now!"

"Did someone say 'back-up'?"

Nya couldn't believe her ears. She wheeled around. The ninja were soaring towards the tower on their elemental dragons!

"Boy, am I glad to see you guys!" she cried. **"Attack!"**
The ghosts seethed. "It's the ninja!" their leader cried.

The ghosts howled and stormed the ninja. Zane swooped in first, shooting ice

blasts to stall them. **"Nya, catch!"** he yelled.

Zane dropped a rope down to Nya. She grabbed it just as three ghosts dived in to knock her off the tower. In a flash, she swung up to join Zane on his dragon.

"Thanks, Zane!" Nya grinned. "I was on some thin ice there!"

"Nya!" Jay called. "Are you okay?"

"I am now!" Nya called back. "What do you say we show these ghosts what we can do as a team?"

"You got it!" Jay cheered. *"Ninja-GO!"*

With a few quick moves, the ninja and their dragons had their enemies surrounded. Since Cole was already a ghost and couldn't be possessed, he grabbed one of the ghost's chains and swung it around the entire group. With a blast of lightning, Jay electrified it, turning it into an electric fence!

The ghosts squirmed. "You fools – this cannot hold us!"

"Perhaps not, but this will," said Zane. He built a cone of ice around the ghosts, trapping them inside.

"What do you say, Sensei?" Kai called to Lloyd.

Lloyd winked. "I'd say it's teatime!"

Kai turned to Nya. "You ready, sis?"

Nya beamed. "You know it!"

With a blast of fire power, Kai melted the ice chamber Zane had created. Nya closed her eyes and concentrated. She felt Kai's, Cole's, Zane's, Lloyd's and Jay's strength surrounding her. **Together, the ninja were unstoppable.**

Tapping into her true potential, Nya commanded the water from the melting ice to swirl around the ghosts. A tornado of water surrounded them. A moment later, the ghosts vanished in an enormous green cloud of smoke.

"We will return!" their leader cried as it disappeared.

Clang. The chain dropped to the tower roof, no longer possessed.

The ninja were left standing alone among the fading green mist.

Nya smiled at her friends. "And we'll be ready if they ever do."

That weekend, the ninja watched as the kids at Ninjago Children's Hospital competed in the video game tournament to determine the ultimate "Ninja for a Day".

"I must say, these children are quite good at the games," Zane noted amid the cheers, chatter and general excitement.

"Yeah, they're killin' it!" Jay said. "Especially little Timmy. He's won every round of *Delivery Trucks vs. Zombies*. He's a kid after my own heart."

Kai joined them. "What do you say we

play a round against the kids, ninja versus 'Ninja for a Day'?"

"I'm in!" exclaimed Cole, chomping on a pizza slice. "Nothing like a tournament to work up an appetite!"

As Cole, Jay, Kai and Zane got started, Nya watched from a nearby refreshment table. Lloyd joined her.

"How's it going here, Nya?" he asked.

"It's going great!" Nya said. "This event really is cheering up the children." Then she was quiet for a moment. "Lloyd, can I ask you something? As a sensei?"

"Sure," said Lloyd.

"Was I wrong to go off on my own all those times?" Nya had told the ninja about all her misadventures. Although she'd been worried about what they'd say, the ninja hadn't judged her or even been mad. They were mostly just glad she was okay.

But Nya couldn't help feeling a bit foolish

for all the trouble she'd got herself into. "Maybe I'm not as strong as I think I am," she confided to Lloyd.

Lloyd shook his head. "I don't think that's true. In fact, I'm pretty sure you're stronger than you think you are. **Because you have us.**"

He paused thoughtfully. "When I was training to be the Green Ninja, I kept telling myself it was up to me to reach my full power. But then I realized I can never reach it, because as long as I have you guys, there's always more to achieve. The team makes me stronger. And I think it's the same for you."

Nya grinned. "Thanks, Lloyd. You really are becoming a sensei."

Lloyd shrugged. "What can I say? I have great teachers."

Nya lined up six ninja action figures side by side on the refreshment table. A mini Cole, Jay, Kai, Lloyd and Zane, plus herself. **"The best,"** she said.

IT TAKES A NINJA... TO WRITE ABOUT A NINJA!

LEGO® and Scholastic are proud to announce the winners of the "Write Like a Ninja" contest!

Kids like you wrote the two stories you're about to read. A jury from LEGO and Scholastic picked these two grand-prize winners out of nearly a thousand submissions.

So congratulations to abbeadventerous114 and JayZX535 . . . and happy reading!

"Write Like a Ninja" Contest
Grand-Prizewinning Story:
"Forgive Me"
by abbeadventerous114

walked silently through the forest surrounding my father's monastery, the imminent storm blocking all light from the sun. I didn't care. It had only been a week since we defeated the Anacondrai. Everyone – and everything – was at peace. All except for me. I had lost my father that day. He was banished to the Cursed Realm so that Chen and his Anacondrai army could be stopped. It worked, but at the cost of his life. I never thought my life could be so empty without him. He isn't down in the training hall when I get up. He isn't there to encourage

IT TAKES A NINJA... TO WRITE ABOUT A NINJA!

LEGO® and Scholastic are proud to announce the winners of the "Write Like a Ninja" contest!

Kids like you wrote the two stories you're about to read. A jury from LEGO and Scholastic picked these two grand-prize winners out of nearly a thousand submissions.

So congratulations to abbeadventerous114 and JayZX535 . . . and happy reading!

"Write Like a Ninja" Contest Grand-Prizewinning Story:

"Forgive Me"
by abbeadventerous114

walked silently through the forest surrounding my father's monastery, the imminent storm blocking all light from the sun. I didn't care. It had only been a week since we defeated the Anacondrai. Everyone – and everything – was at peace. All except for me. I had lost my father that day. He was banished to the Cursed Realm so that Chen and his Anacondrai army could be stopped. It worked, but at the cost of his life. I never thought my life could be so empty without him. He isn't down in the training hall when I get up. He isn't there to encourage me to train. He isn't there when I go to help Cyrus Borg in the afternoon, and he isn't there when I return at night. He was more than my father, more than my sensei. He was my friend. My best friend. I stopped walking and blinked back tears. It wasn't fair.

Rolls of thunder echoed through the valley, and flashes of lightning filled the sky with white light. I began my walk back to the monastery when I heard footsteps behind me. My heart pounded as I spun around and scanned the area for spies.

"Who's there?" I called.

The stranger stepped out of the shadows, his grey hair whipping in the fierce storm winds. Were my eyes playing tricks on me? Or was it real? *It can't be*... I thought fearfully.

"Hello, Lloyd," he said. His voice calmed the storm, and time itself froze. I gasped and took a step back.

"Dad?" I asked.

"Everything will be all right . . ." he said.

"What is going on?" I questioned, taking a step towards him, but he only seemed further away. "Okay, this is crazy!" I stopped dead in my tracks. "You're banished, trapped in the Cursed Realm forever – how are you here? And what do you mean by 'everything will be all right'?" All the anger I had within erupted like a volcano. "Did you even think how banishing yourself would affect us? Mum needs you! I need you, Dad! You were my best friend . . ." I felt my anger subside. It was replaced by sorrow. "You're probably not even really here . . . It's just my mind tricking me," I said quietly, looking down at the grass. "If I could redo what happened that day, I would. I wouldn't have yelled at you, then stormed off . . . I would have said I am sorry for never listening to you. And I would have told you how much you mean to me . . ."

After what seemed like forever, he took

for all the trouble she'd got herself into. "Maybe I'm not as strong as I think I am," she confided to Lloyd.

Lloyd shook his head. "I don't think that's true. In fact, I'm pretty sure you're stronger than you think you are. **Because you have us.**"

He paused thoughtfully. "When I was training to be the Green Ninja, I kept telling myself it was up to me to reach my full power. But then I realized I can never reach it, because as long as I have you guys, there's always more to achieve. The team makes me stronger. And I think it's the same for you."

Nya grinned. "Thanks, Lloyd. You really are becoming a sensei."

Lloyd shrugged. "What can I say? I have great teachers."

Nya lined up six ninja action figures side by side on the refreshment table. A mini Cole, Jay, Kai, Lloyd and Zane, plus herself. **"The best,"** she said.

a step forward and placed his hand on my shoulder. "Lloyd," he said. "Look at me."

I lifted my head and met his eyes.

"I forgive you. And I hope you will forgive me. It was a hard decision, but it needed to be done ... but I promise you, you will see me again." The smallest of smiles formed on his lips.

"But how?" I asked.

"You'll just have to wait and see ..." he said mysteriously. He removed his hand from my shoulder and stepped back. "It's time ..."

"Time for what?" I asked.

"Lloyd, wake up," he said as he began to fade from my vision.

"Wait, Dad!" I called, reaching for him as everything went dark.

"Dad!" I cried out, sitting up. I looked around frantically, my heart pounding. I wasn't in the

Forest of Tranquillity; I was in my bedroom in the monastery. It was all a dream.

There was a soft knock on the door as my mother poked her head in.

"Lloyd, are you all right? I heard a shout from your room . . ." she said.

"I'm fine, Mum . . ." I said, smiling. "Everything will be all right." She nodded and left, closing the door behind her.

I looked at the family photo on my nightstand, focused on my dad, and smiled.

"Thanks, Dad . . ." I said quietly. "I forgive you."

An ever-so-familiar feeling came over me, filling every inch of my body as I lay back down. It was a feeling I hadn't felt in what seemed like ages. Peace. I was at peace. With my father. With what happened. With myself.

I fell asleep that night knowing that one day, I would see my father again.

"Write Like a Ninja" Contest
Grand-Prizewinning Story:
"Wake Up"
by JayZX535

The sheer normalcy of the morning was striking. There had been no calls for help, no attacks and no danger to speak of.

Everything was quiet — almost too quiet. Quiet, that is, except for the game room of the *Destiny's Bounty*...

"Hey! Not fair!" Jay protested. "You can't just gang up on people like that!" He mashed the buttons on his controller as his character lost health.

"Yes, we can," Kai said. "And because you're the biggest gamer out of all of us —

hey! Cole, we were supposed to be fighting Jay!"

"No one said we had to." Cole laughed, but his eyebrows shot up as Kai activated a special move, knocking his character off the screen. "Hey!"

Oddly, the sensei had not appeared to protest, and they went on with their game until at last even video games ceased to be interesting, and the ninja found themselves sitting in boredom.

A long, awkward silence followed. This had never happened before – usually they didn't have much chance to play video games without something coming up. Now, in this uncanny absence of activity, they found themselves at an utter loss.

"Well this is . . . odd," Kai muttered at last. Like the others, he almost expected an alarm to ring even as he spoke, but none did.

"Let's go find the sensei," Cole suggested

after another pause. "This . . . this is too quiet. Something's wrong."

They stood and hurried onto the deck, but the *Bounty* was deserted. Sensei Wu, Nya and Misako were gone.

"What?" Lloyd breathed. "Where . . . where are they?"

"Someone must have taken them!" Zane exclaimed. "Yet how or where I do not know!"

"We need to think," Kai said. "Who could have done this? And how did they get on board while the *Bounty* was in the air?"

"They could have got on the last time we landed," Jay pointed out, "and slipped off again without being noticed."

"Set the coordinates back to our last stopping point," Cole commanded. "Turn the *Bounty* around!"

In minutes, the ship was retracing its route through the sky while Cole phoned the local police department.

"No, sir, we haven't seen them," the officer answered. "But we'll keep looking."

Cole nodded, and then hesitated. "Have you had a quiet day?" he asked, frowning thoughtfully.

"Indeed, we have. No other calls."

"All right, thank you," Cole said. "Call us if you find anything." He put down the phone and stood, returning to the others. "Something's going on here," he said. "I just talked to the police. Get this – they haven't had a single call today!"

"But that makes no sense. Even if we're not called in, there's always something for the police to address!" Jay protested.

"I know," Cole replied, rubbing his forehead. "It all feels so . . . unreal . . ."

"Maybe it *is* unreal," Kai said suddenly.

The others stared at him.

"Kai . . . what are you saying?" Zane asked, perplexed.

"Think about it!" Kai replied quickly. "Everyone but us is missing, yet the *Bounty* has been in the air for hours. And am I the only one who recalls seeing them after we last took off?"

The others hesitated. Now that Kai mentioned it, all of them *did* remember seeing the rest of the team after they'd taken flight.

"But . . . that's impossible!" Lloyd replied. "This doesn't make sense!"

"Exactly," Kai replied, "It's not possible! None of this is real!"

As soon as the words had left his mouth, the air around them shimmered, dissolving into mist. They found themselves lying on the deck of the *Bounty*, staring up at a hooded figure.

"The Dreamweaver," Cole breathed. "Of course! He used his powers to trap us in a dream so we couldn't stop him!"

The hooded man glared down at them.

"How did you do that? No one escapes my dreams!"

"A ninja must see what others do not," Zane said, rising to his feet along with the others. "And your evil deeds have gone unchecked for far too long!"

The Dreamweaver stepped back, eyes darting to each of the ninja in turn. The teammates exchanged glances.

"I think it's clear what we need to do," Kai said, and the others nodded.

Then, as one, they raised their voices –

"*Ninja-GO!*"